Jack and the Beanstalk

In memory of Richard Walker

For my Grandparents
May and Grania
and in memory of
Richard and Joe — *N.S.*

Barefoot Books
124 Walcot Street
Bath
BA1 5BG

Text copyright © 1999 by Richard Walker
Illustrations copyright © 1999 by Niamh Sharkey

The moral right of Richard Walker to be identified as the author and
Niamh Sharkey to be identified as the illustrator of this work has been asserted

The illustrations were prepared in oil and gesso on canvas
This book was typeset in Monotype Bembo Bold 20pt on 32pt leading

Graphic design by Design/Section, Frome
Colour separation by Grafiscan, Verona
Printed and bound in Singapore by Tien Wah Press (Pte) Ltd

This book has been printed on 100% acid-free paper

Hardback ISBN 1 901223 61 2
Paperback ISBN 1 901223 37 X

British Cataloguing-in-Publication Data: a catalogue
record for this book is available from the British Library

7 9 8 6

Jack
and the
Beanstalk

retold by
Richard Walker

illustrated by
Niamh Sharkey

Barefoot Books
Celebrating Art and Story

*I'm not going to start by saying
that Jack was lazy. When there
was an adventure in the offing,
he was not lazy at all. But
most of the time, he just
did a little bit of this and
a little bit of that.*

Jack lived with his mum and Daisy, the cow, in
a tumbledown farmhouse, a little way out of town.
Jack's mum liked to do just a little bit of this and
a little bit of that as well. They didn't have very
much money, but they didn't much care.

Then one day
there was nothing
left to eat, not even
a crust of old bread,
and no money left
either to buy anything.

'It's no good, Jack,' his mum said. 'We'll have
to sell poor old Daisy. You had better get up
early tomorrow morning and take her to market.
Make sure you get a good price for her!'

Jack knew better than to argue. Besides, he was very hungry. So the next day he got up at sunrise and set off down the lane with Daisy in tow.

He had not gone far when he came
around a corner and bumped into a funny
little man. The man was wearing a big,
baggy jacket with big, baggy pockets.

'Good morning to you!' said the man.
'That's a nice-looking cow
you have there. Do you
fancy doing a swap
for her?'

Jack remembered what his mum had told him, so he asked, 'What will you give me in exchange?'

'These!' declared the funny little man and, plunging a hand deep into one of his pockets, he pulled out six plump beans.

'Those?' asked Jack.

'Yes,' said the funny little man, 'these! Don't think these are just ordinary beans. Oh no! These are magic beans. But you will have to be careful with them. I've lost the instructions for them, so I'm not sure what they do.'

Well, there was nothing Jack loved better than magic, so he handed over Daisy, took the beans and hurried home.

As soon as he reached the back door, Jack burst into the kitchen and proudly threw the beans down on the table.

'What's this?' exclaimed his mum.

'Oh dear,' thought Jack.

'They're magic beans, Mum. I swapped
them for Daisy. At least we've got something
to eat…well, we will have when they've grown.'
Jack's mum was furious. She went white
in the face and shouted and stamped.
Then she threw open the window
and flung the beans outside.
That night, Jack and his
mum went to bed
feeling miserable
and hungry.

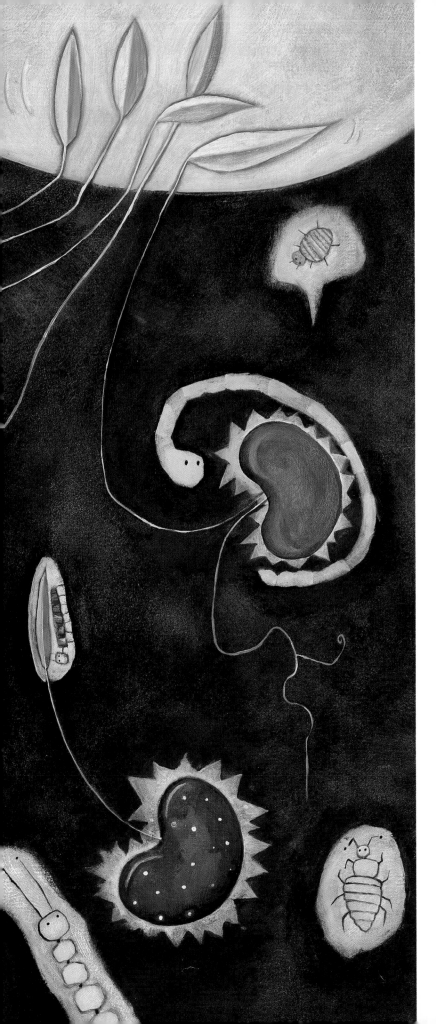

But in the garden,
things began to
happen. The beans
slipped down through
cracks in the ground.
Their roots wriggled
deep into the earth
and shoots pushed
upwards. They burst
through the hard
crust of the soil
and, twisting and
tangling together,
they grew high into
the sky. They kept
on growing and
growing until they
reached the land of
the clouds.

Then a long, wiry tendril reached down to the house and tapped on Jack's bedroom window.

'Who's that?' Jack yawned. He saw strange shadows in the moonlit window and, not sure whether this was a dream or a real adventure, he padded across the room and drew back his curtains. There, bending and swaying in the moonlight, was the most enormous beanstalk he had ever seen.

'I wonder where the top of it goes to?' Jack said to himself.

There was only one way to find out. Without stopping to think twice, he clambered over the windowsill and started to climb. Soon the house was just a tiny dot, far below. Still he made his way upwards.

Finally he reached the land of the clouds and
stepped off the beanstalk on to the fluffy grey
ground. In the distance, he could see a huge
castle. Jack walked straight up to it and knocked
on the door. He heard the clank of keys being

turned, the rumble of bars being slid back and
the rattle of chains being unfastened. Then, at
last, the huge door creaked open a crack and he
saw a little old woman peering at him by the
light of a candle.

'You can't come in!' she whispered. 'He'll be back soon.

GO AWAY!'

'Please!' Jack begged. 'I'm a stranger here and starving hungry. Can't I just pop in quickly for something to eat?'

The woman looked at him more closely and saw that he was a nice-looking lad with a ready smile.

'Very well, you can come in for a minute,' she said, 'but don't let him catch sight of you.'

'Who's *he*?' asked Jack as they made their way along the dusty castle corridors to the big kitchen. Lining the walls were mounds of huge, bulging sacks, which jingled as Jack brushed against them.

'The giant, of course. If he catches you, he'll eat you for sure. He's got a foul temper so you'd better keep out of his way. Hide among the sacks if you hear him coming.'

Then, just as she finished speaking, there was a crashing of heavy footsteps outside the room. Jack only just managed to hide behind a heap of sacks when the door burst open and in barged the giant.

'FEE, FI, FO, FUM!

...I smell the blood of a stinky man! Where is he, woman? Where are you hiding him?' The giant sniffled his way round the room until he came close to where Jack was hiding.

'Oh, don't be silly!' said the old woman. 'All you can smell is the stew I've made. I was trying a bowl of it to make sure it was good enough for you. Would you like some?'

Soon the giant had slurped his way through an enormous bowl of stew. He belched loudly, then demanded, 'Fetch me my goose! I want some more gold!'

The old woman slipped out of the room and was soon back, cradling a huge, very gloomy-looking bird in her arms. Peeping out from his hiding place, Jack watched as the goose began to lay eggs — each one made of pure gold. As each egg appeared, the giant put it into a giant egg box. Then he demanded, 'Now fetch me my harp. I want some music!'

Once again, the old woman bustled out of the room and came back holding an exquisite harp made of pure gold. Even the strings were golden. 'Play, harp, play!' shouted the giant... And, as if by magic, the room was filled with

the most beautiful, gentle music as the strings began to vibrate all by themselves. Soon the giant fell asleep and his snuffling and snoring echoed round the room.

Jack crept out from his hiding place and quietly began to drag one of the bulging sacks, full of gold coins, across the kitchen floor. It was very heavy and it jingled as he pulled it, but the giant did not stir. Jack heaved and heaved and dragged the sack right out of the castle, across the cloud and back to the top of the beanstalk. The sack was too heavy for him to carry any further so he left it there and slid quickly down.

When he reached home, Jack found his mum staring up at the beanstalk and scratching her head. 'Rope!' cried Jack as he sprang to the ground. He ran off to the shed and came back a few moments later with great coils wrapped round him. Then he set off back up the beanstalk.

At the top of the beanstalk, Jack tied one end of the rope to the stem and the other to the sack of gold. Then he started to lower the sack.

After a while, he felt the rope become loose, and he knew that the sack had reached the ground safely and that his mum had untied it.

Jack headed back to the kitchen to fetch another sack. As he crept past the giant, the goose looked up hopefully and whispered, 'Can I come too? I hate it up here. You wouldn't need to take the sack then. I could lay you as many golden eggs as you want.'

So Jack picked her up and ran out of the room. In the corridor, he bumped into the old woman.

'Can I come with you as well?' she asked.
'Of course,' said Jack. 'Here, you take the
goose and I'll go back for the harp.'

But as Jack picked up the harp, it
suddenly cried out, 'What's going on?
Who are you? Help! Help!' Jack raced
out of the kitchen just as the giant woke up,
saw what was happening and began to give chase.
Faster and faster ran Jack. Closer and closer came
the giant.

As he reached the top of the beanstalk, Jack could
feel the giant's hand on the hairs of his neck.

'Quick!' he shouted.

The old woman started
slithering down with the
goose. Jack slithered down
behind her with the harp.
They could hear the giant
shouting and swearing as
he tried to follow them.

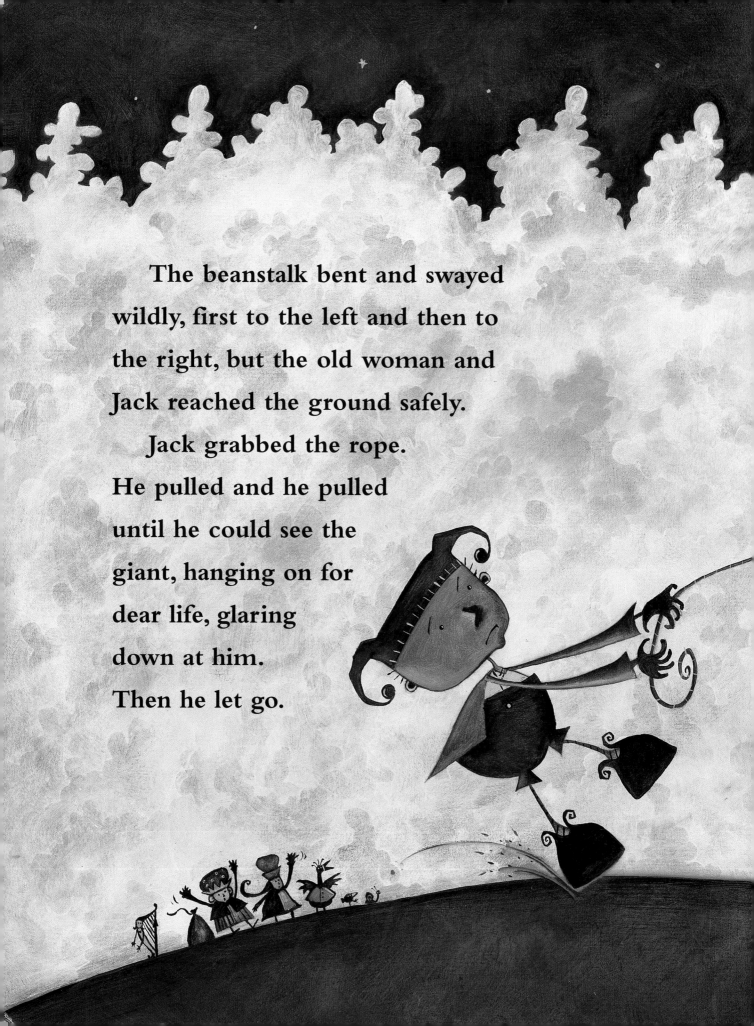

The beanstalk bent and swayed
wildly, first to the left and then to
the right, but the old woman and
Jack reached the ground safely.

Jack grabbed the rope.
He pulled and he pulled
until he could see the
giant, hanging on for
dear life, glaring
down at him.
Then he let go.

GG!

The beanstalk shot upright
like an enormous catapult. Unable
to hold on any longer, the giant flew
off the end. He soared away into space
and was never seen again. And, as
far as I know, he's still there.

The old woman went inside to make a pot of tea. Mum put the golden harp on the kitchen dresser, and Jack made the magic goose a special hut. He put the sack of gold in the cellar and took out a coin whenever he needed to buy something. And the last time I went to visit, the harp played jigs and reels, so we all had a merry dance.